Robin Hood
and the
Golden Arrow

by Elizabeth Dale and Isabel Muñoz

W
FRANKLIN WATTS
LONDON • SYDNEY

Chapter 1

Long, long ago in Sherwood Forest, there lived a famous man called Robin Hood. He and his band of merry men roamed the forest. They dressed in green so they could hide more easily amongst the trees.

They spent their days hunting deer and practising fighting and archery. But, most importantly, they robbed all the rich people who came through the forest, and gave the money to the poor. Robin was known across the land. He had many exciting adventures, outwitting his enemy, the Sheriff of Nottingham. One of his most famous adventures began with an event one spring afternoon ...

It was a beautiful sunny day in Sherwood Forest. A rich lord in a flowing red cape was riding along the shady path, smiling to himself. He'd just made a lot of money and had eaten a big lunch.

Suddenly ...

Whoosh!

An arrow flew through the air, skimming his head and sending his hat flying.

"What ... how ... ?" The lord looked around, terrified. Then he saw the famous archer, dressed all in green.

"R ... R ... Robin H ... Hood!" he stuttered.

"Hello, there!" smiled Robin. "Worry not, my fine fellow, I'm here to help. Your poor horse looks tired, so let me lighten her load. Hand me your heavy moneybags and your jewellery and gold chains."

Reluctantly, the rich lord did as Robin said.

"You'll suffer for this!" he said, scowling. "I'll tell the Sheriff."

"Please do!" laughed Robin. "Tell him that yet again I have robbed a rich man to give his money to the poor."

The Sheriff was furious when he heard the news. His solders quaked in their boots as the Sheriff ranted and shouted. "That man's forever robbing noblemen!" he cried. "I must devise a plan to catch him. Who will help me?"

One of the soldiers stepped forward. "Sire," he said, his voice quaking with fear. "I have an idea."

When he heard the plan, the Sheriff's eyes lit up.

Chapter 2

One day, when Robin was out hunting deer,

he saw a poster nailed to the Greenwood Tree.

'Win a Golden Arrow' it read.

"What fun!" laughed Robin. "The Sheriff is

holding a competition at Nottingham Castle

to find the best archer in the country. I'm sure

I can win. I'm one of the best archers in the land."

But Robin's men were worried.

9

"Master Robin, this competition might be a trap," said Will. "As soon as you enter the castle grounds, the Sheriff's men will be sure to capture you." "But I have to go," insisted Robin. "Or he'll call me a coward for not daring to show my face." His men disagreed. The risk was too great.

"We couldn't bear it if you were captured," they said. "You're our leader."

"And I always will be," said Robin. "I've tricked the Sheriff many times and will do again. Don't worry, I have a plan, and I will need you all to help me."

Chapter 3

On the day of the competition, crowds gathered

from far and wide. Rich people, dressed in their

best clothes, mingled with poor woodsmen and

beggars.

Brightly coloured tents covered the field, with flags and bunting fluttering in the breeze. There was a great sense of excitement as the people waited for the competition to begin. Finally, the Sheriff arrived and took his seat.

"Hmm, I cannot see Robin Hood yet," he thought, peering at all the archers. "As the weaker archers get knocked out and the group gets smaller it will be easier to spot his blonde hair and green clothes."

It was a hard competition. The target was
150 metres from the archers, and many missed it
altogether. Others were brilliant and the people
cheered on their favourites. Then one archer hit
the bulls-eye and the crowd roared!

After the first round, only the ten best archers
were left in the competition. The Sheriff studied
them closely. He recognised eight of the men,
including Gill the Red Cap and Adam of the Dell.
But there was a stranger in blue, who was too thin
to be Robin, and a tattered beggar dressed
in scarlet. The beggar wore a patch over one eye
and had brown hair whereas Robin's was gold.
So Robin hadn't come! The Sheriff was furious.

15

The best three archers went forward to the final round – they were Gill the Red Cap, the beggar in scarlet, and Adam of the Dell. Everyone shouted out the name of their favourite and the noise was deafening. But no one cheered for the beggar in scarlet.

Three more shots would decide the winner. The crowds went quiet. Everyone was tense as, one after the other, each archer pulled back his string and shot his arrow. Every one hit the target. But the last shot of all, fired by the beggar in scarlet, hit the bulls-eye. Now the crowd did clap and cheer for him. He was the clear winner.

The Sheriff was delighted. "Well done!" he said,

presenting the golden arrow to the beggar.

"What is your name, my good man?"

"Jock of Teviot," replied the archer.

"Well, Jock, you're a brilliant archer,"

the Sheriff declared. "Far better than that

coward Robin Hood who dared not show his face

today. Will you join my service? I'll pay you well."

"No, my lord, I thank you," the beggar replied,
"I'm my own man and will work for no one else,
no matter who."

The Sheriff was annoyed at being turned down
in front of so many people.

"Then go now!" he snapped, "before I beat you
for your insolence!"

Chapter 4

That evening, such a strange group of woodsmen and beggars gathered around the Greenwood Tree in Sherwood Forest. Together they removed their disguises to reveal their green clothes underneath, for they were Robin Hood's merry men. They all laughed and clapped each other on the back to think of the fun they'd had that day. But the biggest cheer of all was for the beggar who took off his eye-patch and scarlet rags. For he was ... Robin Hood!

"Clothes come off easily," said Robin Hood,
"but I'm afraid the walnut stain will be harder
to remove from my yellow hair and beard."
Everyone laughed and cheered.

"The Sheriff looked me in the eye so hard as he
presented the prize, I felt sure he would recognise
me and clap me in chains," said Robin. "But
instead he gave me this golden arrow and offered
me a job!"

Everyone laughed even more to think how Robin,
with his clever disguise, had fooled the Sheriff.

That night in the forest there was a huge feast to celebrate. Robin was proud and happy that he had won the competition – even with one blind eye. Just one thing spoiled his evening.

He took his good friend Little John aside.

"Everyone heard the Sheriff say that the beggar was a far better shot than Robin Hood who had been too cowardly to come," he said. "I have to let the Sheriff know I'm not a coward. How can I prove to him that I was there at the competition – and that it was I who won the golden arrow?"

"Worry not, Master Robin," replied Little John, with a smile. "I will attend to this immediately."

Chapter 5

Little John rode straight to Nottingham. As he
reached the castle, he could hear the singing and
laughter as the Sheriff and his friends celebrated
together.

"Let's drink a toast!" said the Sheriff, raising his
tankard. "Friends, Lords and Noblemen. I didn't
capture Robin Hood today, but I have shamed him
in front of everyone. No more will he be able to
hold his head up high or strike fear in our hearts.
For everyone now knows he is nothing but a great
big coward!"

But just at that moment, something flew through the open window. The Sheriff ducked as an arrow whistled past him, narrowly missing his ear and landing amongst the dishes. The noise made everyone jump. On the end of the arrow was tied a scroll. Shakily, the Sheriff unrolled it. He went bright red and shook with rage as he read aloud:

"Now Heaven bless Thy Grace this day
Say all in sweet Sherwood.
For you did give the prize away
To merry Robin Hood."

"No!" cried the Sheriff. Once more Robin Hood
had made a fool of him. But never again.

The Sheriff banged the table. "That's it!" he cried.
"Robin Hood has gone too far this time! Come on,
men! We need to start planning our next trap.
I vow I'll catch that man if it's the last thing I do!"

Things to think about

1. Why does the Sheriff want to capture Robin Hood?
2. Why does Robin want to enter the archery competition?
3. What makes Robin and his men think it could be a trap?
4. How does Robin manage to enter the competition without getting caught?
5. How does the Sheriff feel at the end of the story? Do you think the Sheriff will try to catch Robin again?

Write it yourself

One of the themes in this story is tricking someone.
Now try to write your own story with a similar theme.
Plan your story before you begin to write it.
Start off with a story map:

• a beginning to introduce the characters and where and when your story is set (the setting);

• a problem that the main characters will need to fix in the story;

• an ending where the problems are resolved.

Get writing! Create a story that reverses a trick of some kind, so that the person who first set the trick, is in turn tricked! Think carefully about who your heroes and villains will be.

Notes for parents and carers

Independent reading

The aim of independent reading is to read this book with ease. This series is designed to provide an opportunity for your child to read for pleasure and enjoyment. These notes are written for you to help your child make the most of this book.

About the book

Robin Hood wants to prove he is the best archer in the land, so when he sees an archery competition he simply must enter! However, he knows the Sheriff of Nottingham will be out to catch him, so he devises a cunning disguise!

Before reading

Ask your child why they have selected this book. Look at the title and blurb together. What do they think it will be about? Do they think they will like it?

During reading

Encourage your child to read independently. If they get stuck on a longer word, remind them that they can find syllable chunks that can be sounded out from left to right. They can also read on in the sentence and think about what would make sense.

After reading

Support comprehension by talking about the story. What happened?
Then help your child think about the messages in the book that go beyond the story, using the questions on the page opposite. Give your child a chance to respond to the story, asking:
Did you enjoy the story and why? Who was your favourite character?
What was your favourite part? What did you expect to happen at the end?

Franklin Watts
First published in Great Britain in 2019
by The Watts Publishing Group

Series Editors: Jackie Hamley and Melanie Palmer
Series Advisors: Dr Sue Bodman and Glen Franklin
Series Designer: Peter Scoulding

A CIP catalogue record for this book is
available from the British Library.

ISBN 978 1 4451 6344 4 (hbk)
ISBN 978 1 4451 6346 8 (pbk)
ISBN 978 1 4451 6345 1 (library ebook)

Printed in China

Franklin Watts
An imprint of
Hachette Children's Group
Part of The Watts Publishing Group
Carmelite House
50 Victoria Embankment
London EC4Y 0DZ

An Hachette UK Company
www.hachette.co.uk

www.franklinwatts.co.uk